EDGE BOOKS™

The Unexplained

ATLANTIS

by **Michael Martin**

Consultant:
Curtis Runnels, PhD
Professor of Archaeology
Department of Archaeology, Boston University
Boston, Massachusetts

Capstone *press*®
Mankato, Minnesota

Edge Books are published by Capstone Press,
151 Good Counsel Drive, P.O. Box 669, Mankato, Minnesota 56002.
www.capstonepress.com

Library of Congress Cataloging-in-Publication Data
Martin, Michael, 1948–
    Atlantis / by Michael Martin.
       p. cm.—(Edge books. The unexplained)
    Summary: "Describes the lost continent of Atlantis and theories
about its possible location"—Provided by publisher.
    Includes bibliographical references and index.
    ISBN–13: 978-0-7368-6759-7 (hardcover)
    ISBN–10: 0-7368-6759-7 (hardcover)
    1. Atlantis—Juvenile literature. I. Title.
GN751.M33 2007
001.94—dc22   2006024061

Editorial Credits
Aaron Sautter, editor; Juliette Peters, set designer; Patrick D. Dentinger, book designer;
    Scott Thoms, illustrator; Deirdre Barton, photo researcher/photo editor

Photo Credits
Corbis/epa/WEDA, 18; Gianni Dagli Orti, 6, 21; Jim Zuckerman, 20;
    Kevin Schafer, 26; zefa/José Fuste Raga, 15
Fortean Picture Library, 5, 11, 25, 27; Frank Joseph, 29
Getty Images Inc./Iconica/Sergio Pitamitz, 13 (bottom); The Image Bank/
    Antonio M. Rosario, cover
iStockphoto Inc./Gregory Albertini, 8 (back middle); Sue Colvil, 8 (front middle)
Mary Evans Picture Library, 23, 24
Shutterstock/Andre Klaassen, 13 (top); Andy Lim, 8 (top right); Hiroshi Sato, 8
    (background); Michael Shake, 8 (bottom right, bottom left); WH Chow, 17

1 2 3 4 5 6 12 11 10 09 08 07

TABLE OF CONTENTS

FEATURES

Chapter 1

THE LEGEND OF ATLANTIS

Around 360 BC, Greek scholar Plato wrote a story about a mysterious island nation. It was a large island, and its people were very advanced. But in one night, the island and its people disappeared into the Atlantic Ocean.

Plato said he learned about the island from an ancient story. In 600 BC, a famous Greek named Solon visited Egypt. There, Solon heard about the sinking of a great island thousands of years before. The island's name was Atlantis. He brought the story back to Greece. Eventually, Plato heard about Atlantis and decided to write the story down.

Learn about:
• An ancient mystery
• A lost civilization
• The Temple of Poseidon

Plato said the capital city of Atlantis was filled with beautiful buildings covered in gold and silver.

Some people think Plato made up the story of Atlantis to show what can happen if a society becomes too powerful.

An Impressive Civilization

Plato wrote that the island of Atlantis was about 230 miles (370 kilometers) wide and 340 miles (550 kilometers) long. He said the island was located beyond the Pillars of Hercules. Today, this narrow sea passage is called the Strait of Gibraltar. It connects the Mediterranean Sea with the Atlantic Ocean.

Plato also said Atlantis had an advanced civilization. The people were wealthy and powerful. Many were master shipbuilders and sailors. They traded goods with other cultures in Europe and Africa. Their buildings were plated with bronze and silver and roofed with gold.

The capital city was a marvel of engineering. Canals were arranged in rings around the city. Large tunnels allowed ships to pass from one canal to the other. The city was filled with beautiful palaces, harbors, and temples. The huge Temple of Poseidon sat on top of a hill near the city's center.

The Temple of Poseidon

Plato gave detailed descriptions of the Temple of Poseidon. The temple was 600 feet (180 meters) long and 300 feet (90 meters) wide. The outside of the temple sparkled and shimmered in the sunlight. The walls were covered with silver, and the roof peaks were made of gold. The ceiling inside the temple was made of carved ivory.

Gold statues of Atlantis' 10 kings stood throughout the temple. The largest and most impressive statue was of Poseidon, the god of the sea. His head reached nearly to the ceiling. He held the reins of a chariot that was pulled by six winged horses. Every five to six years, the 10 kings of Atlantis met at the temple to discuss the island's affairs and perform religious rituals.

Plato wrote that the first king of Atlantis was Atlas. According to Plato, the island and city of Atlantis were named after Atlas, as was the Atlantic Ocean.

The Last Days

According to Plato, the Atlanteans began to believe they were better than other people. They started wars with other countries and conquered lands as far east as Egypt. They even made slaves of their prisoners.

Plato's story says the Atlanteans tried to attack the city of Athens in Greece, but failed. Soon after, huge earthquakes hit the island. Giant tidal waves rolled across the land. The island and its people were buried beneath the sea forever.

Chapter 2

SEARCHING FOR ATLANTIS

For more than 2,000 years, people have wondered if Atlantis was a real place. Today, many believe Plato made up the story to teach a lesson about powerful and corrupt governments. Even one of Plato's students, Aristotle, said the story was meant to be a fable.

But Plato often stresses in the story that he is talking about real history. And Aristotle's writings on the subject were lost long ago. For these reasons, many people continue to look for the legendary lost city.

Learn about:
• Facts or fables
• Ignatius Donnelly
• Pyramids

If Atlantis was a real place, it might be filled with many treasures just waiting to be found.

The Great Flood

In the late 1800s, U.S. Congressman Ignatius Donnelly made the subject of Atlantis very popular. In 1882, he wrote a book about his ideas on Atlantis. He wrote about how cultures around the world tell stories of a great flood. He believed all the legends were really memories of the same flood that destroyed Atlantis.

Donnelly thought Atlantis survivors might have settled on both sides of the Atlantic Ocean. He believed cultures with similar customs and languages came from Atlantis. He also thought Atlantis survivors built the pyramids found in both Egypt and Central America. But scientists have since found that the pyramids are not as alike as Donnelly thought. They were built during different times in history.

Pyramids in Egypt (top) and Central America (bottom) look similar. But scientists say they were not built by the same culture.

EDGE FACT

Many Atlantic islands, such as the Azores near Spain, are the peaks of underwater volcanic mountain ranges.

Donnelly also thought some Atlantic islands were the mountaintops of Atlantis. The Azore Islands near Spain lie just west of the Strait of Gibralter. Donnelly thought the islands could be the remains of Atlantis. But few scientists agreed with him. They doubted such a large island could just vanish overnight. Today, most believers think that if Atlantis ever existed, other sites are far more likely.

▲ Some people think Atlantic islands, like the Canary Islands near Africa, could be the mountaintops of Atlantis.

15

Chapter 3

THE SANTORINI SOLUTION

Today, many researchers think Plato was mistaken about Atlantis. Perhaps he overstated a smaller natural disaster. Or maybe he was repeating a made-up story someone told him. Despite the doubts, the legend of Atlantis continues to fascinate people.

If Atlantis did exist, the biggest mystery of all is its location. Dozens of sites have been suggested. They include Africa, Spain, Indonesia, and the Canary Islands. One of the most convincing ideas involves the island of Santorini near Greece.

Learn about:
• Suggested locations
• A gigantic explosion
• Crete and the Minoans

Today, Santorini serves as a
popular spot for tourists.

▲ Volcanoes can be extremely powerful. The volcanic blast at Santorini destroyed most of the island.

A Volcano Erupts

The second-most powerful volcanic eruption in recorded history took place around 1600 BC. The volcano on Santorini, then known as Thera, blew up with a blast heard thousands of miles away. Most of the island was destroyed. The blast blew a huge crater in the center of the island. Sea water rushed into the crater, sending tidal waves roaring across the Mediterranean Sea. Tons of thick volcanic ash blackened the skies and buried nearby towns.

Although Santorini's destruction seems to fit Plato's story, the island is too small. But there was a much larger island close by. Crete is 35 miles (56 kilometers) wide and 152 miles (245 kilometers) long. It was also the center of a mysterious, advanced civilization. The Minoan culture on Crete disappeared within about 200 years of the Santorini explosion.

EDGE FACT

The eruption of Santorini is believed to be nearly 20 times more powerful than the 1980 explosion of Mount St. Helens in Washington State.

A Vanished Culture

About 4,000 years ago, the Minoans were one of the most advanced societies in Europe. They built large palaces and temples. They made beautiful pottery and paintings. They even kept written records about their culture. At least 300 tablets have been found with Minoan writing on them.

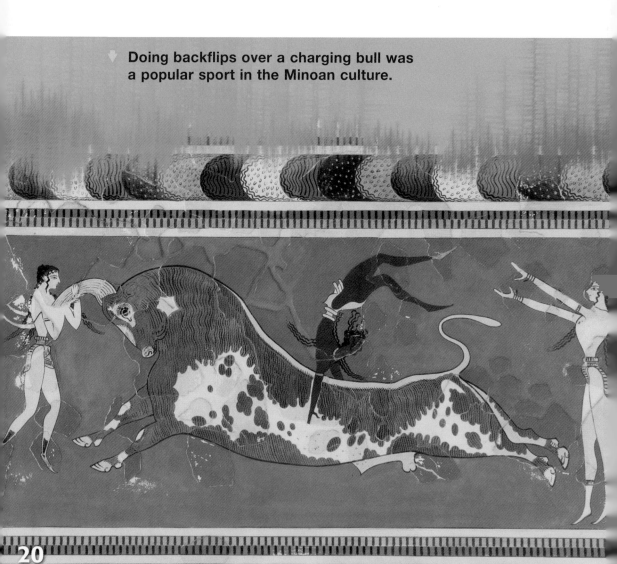

Doing backflips over a charging bull was a popular sport in the Minoan culture.

The large beams and pillars used in the palace at Knossos on Crete shows the Minoans' advanced building methods.

Tidal waves from the Santorini explosion would have hit Crete's coastal towns. Volcanic ash would have rained down on the land. Perhaps Plato combined the Santorini disaster with the Minoan culture to create the Atlantis story.

Chapter 4

OTHER THEORIES

One of the problems in finding Atlantis involves a possible mistake in math. Scientists point out that the Egyptian symbol for 100 looks a lot like the Greek symbol for 1,000. Maybe Plato's numbers were all 10 times too large. If true, then Atlantis would have been a much smaller island. It would also have been destroyed at a much later date. If Plato was mistaken about these things, then perhaps he was also wrong about Atlantis' location. Because of this, people continue to look for Atlantis in other places around the world.

Learn about:
• A possible math mistake
• Edgar Cayce and the Bimini Road
• Atlantis in Antarctica?

Nobody knows what would remain of Atlantis. Many searchers dream of finding the city's buildings intact.

Edgar Cayce and Atlantis

In 1940, psychic Edgar Cayce predicted parts of Atlantis would rise again in 1968 or 1969. He said this would happen somewhere in the Bahama Islands. Cayce died in 1945. But in 1968, a mysterious discovery was made near Bimini Island in the Caribbean Sea. Young archaeologist J. Manson Valentine found an unusual rock formation about 15 feet (4.5 meters) under the water near the island's shore. Two parallel lines of stone blocks stretched about 2,000 feet (610 meters) along the ocean floor.

The formation quickly became known as the Bimini Road. Some people thought the stone blocks could be part of Atlantis. They think it could be an ancient ship harbor. But sometimes beachrock breaks into square-shaped blocks. Most scientists believe the Bimini Road is just a natural rock formation.

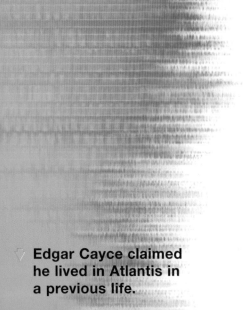

Edgar Cayce claimed he lived in Atlantis in a previous life.

The stone blocks forming the Bimini Road look like people could have made them. But most scientists think it's just a natural rock formation.

An Icy Atlantis

One of the most creative theories about Atlantis was suggested in 1995. Authors Rand and Rose Flem-Ath wrote a book saying that Atlantis was once in Antarctica. They based their idea on the research of professor Charles Hapgood.

▲ Some people think Antarctica might have been home to Atlantis.

During the 1950s, Hapgood studied old sea maps from the 1500s. He thought the maps showed mountains and coastlines of Antarctica. But Antarctica was not officially discovered until the 1800s. Hapgood thought the maps were copied from much older maps made when Antarctica was warmer. The Flem-Aths believe that Atlantis must have existed there during this time. But scientists think their claims are unlikely. Antarctica has been buried under great sheets of ice for millions of years.

Some think the Piri Reis map from 1513 shows Antarctica's coastline.

The Search Goes On

In 2006, researchers exploring the Bimini Road found several odd stones with holes in them. Several of the stones seemed to have grooves where ropes might have been wrapped around them. Similar stones have been found in the Mediterranean Sea. Ancient sailors used stones like these as anchors. But scientists note that some clams and other sea creatures can bore holes through rock too. They aren't convinced the Bimini stones are ancient ship anchors.

Whether the discoveries at Bimini are related to Atlantis is unknown. But people will go on looking for the legendary lost island. The chance of finding the remains of Atlantis is too exciting to give up the search.

Underwater researcher William Donato has studied the Bimini Road for several years.

GLOSSARY

canal (kuh-NAL)—a channel that connects two bodies of water; ships use canals to sail between the bodies of water.

civilization (siv-i-luh-ZAY-shuhn)—an organized and advanced society

culture (KUHL-chur)—a people's way of life, ideas, customs, and traditions

custom (KUHSS-tuhm)—a tradition in a culture or society

eruption (i-RUHPT-shuhn)—a volcano's action of throwing out rock, hot ash, and lava with great force

psychic (SYE-kik)—someone who claims to be able to tell what people are thinking or to predict the future

society (suh-SYE-uh-tee)—a group of people who share the same laws and customs

theory (THIHR-ee)—an idea that explains something that is unknown

READ MORE

Herbst, Judith. *Lands of Mystery*. The Unexplained. Minneapolis: Lerner, 2005.

Joseph, Frank. *The Atlantis Encyclopedia*. Franklin Lakes, N. J.: New Page Books, 2005.

Nardo, Don. *Atlantis*. The Mystery Library. San Diego: Lucent Books, 2004.

INTERNET SITES

FactHound offers a safe, fun way to find Internet sites related to this book. All of the sites on FactHound have been researched by our staff.

Here's how:
1. Visit *www.facthound.com*
2. Choose your grade level.
3. Type in this book ID code **0736867597** for age-appropriate sites. You may also browse subjects by clicking on letters, or by clicking on pictures and words.
4. Click on the **Fetch It** button.

FactHound will fetch the best sites for you!

INDEX